Fey Folk

ALEXANDROS PAPADIAMANDIS

Fey Folk

A tale from Skiathos

Translated by
David Connolly

AIORA

David Connolly was Professor of Translation Studies at the Aristotle University of Thessaloniki and is now retired. He has translated over 50 books with works by contemporary Greek writers. His translations have received prizes in the USA, the UK and Greece.

This translation was first published in *The Boundless Garden, vol. I*, Denise Harvey Publisher (Limni, Evia, 2007) and is reproduced here by kind permission of the publisher.

Photographs in this book were generously provided by the Retired Seamen Association of Skiathos.

Original title: *Οι ελαφροΐσκιωτοι*

First published May 2013
Reprinted April 2023

ISBN: 978-618-5048-06-8

AIORA PRESS
11 Mavromichali st.
Athens 10679 - Greece
tel: +30 210 3839000
www.aiorabooks.com

Contents

Introduction 11

Fey Folk 17

Biographical Note 71

Selected Works in English Translation.................. 75

Introduction

Referred to by George Seferis, Greece's first Nobel Laureate, as "the greatest Modern Greek prose writer", Alexandros Papadiamandis holds a special place in the history of modern Greek Letters, but also in the heart of the ordinary Greek reader. His realistic and sensitive descriptions of rural communities with their customs and traditions and of a village life often characterized by poverty and harshness, estrangement and repressed feelings, yet governed by an underlying and tangibly present divine order have endeared him to generations of Greek readers, both young and old.

Born the son of a village Priest on the island of Skiathos, he spent much of his adult life working in Athens. He could be termed a professional writer in the sense that he wrote for a living, translating a vast number of foreign works and writing his own stories for Athenian newspapers and periodicals. A number of his longer works, like *The Murderess*, were serialized in various newspapers in Dickensian fashion and many of his short stories have a seasonal character precisely because of the demands of the daily and periodic press for which he wrote.

Like many of the more interesting Greek writers in the last decades of the 19th century (Vizyinos, Karkavitsas), Papadiamandis assimilated new trends from abroad, but combined these with an attempt to identify and explore the specific aspects of a perceived notion of Greekness, highlighting folk traditions, customs, manners and the way of life in the Greek countryside. A number of stories are, admittedly, set in Athens where he lived, but the majority of them refer specifically to his native island of Skiathos, as it was always Skiathos and its inhabitants that were in his thoughts, which perhaps accounts for the distinctly nostalgic tone in many of these stories.

Not only do we find vivid, sometimes paradisiacal, descriptions of the landscapes and seascapes of his native island, but nature itself often assumes an active role in his stories. Papadiamandis infuses his portrayal of nature with a dreamlike quality, highlighting the mystery and magic of the world in which human dramas unfold. Nature in his stories is bountiful, maternal and tender, but at times severe and relentless: an instrument of divine providence but also of divine retribution.

Much more, however, than simple portraits of life in small, rural communities and a narration of events there, his stories attempt a subtle exploration of the psychology of his characters. And this combination of acute and sensitive character portrayal together with realistic and compelling descriptions of village life is variously expressed with a mixture of detachment, humour, irony and sympathy. His stories often tend towards the moralistic and didactic, but any moralizing and didacticism is tempered always with deeply human compassion.

In addition to the often moving themes of his stories and their endearing and intriguing characters, another aspect of his work that captivates the Greek reader is the characteristic charm of his language. In this context, Odysseus Elytis, Greece's second Nobel Laureate, talks of the "magic" of Papadiamandis. It is a magic woven using a mixture of linguistic idioms comprising the demotic and purist forms of his times, ecclesiastical Greek and local island dialect, all masterfully superimposed without any strain on the language of the narrative and always tailored to the needs of the story. What, however, exerts a charm on the Greek reader is lost for the most part on the reader in translation, for whom, at best, only a hint of the linguistic tapestry of the original work can be retained. The reader who wishes to explore Papadiamandis's work further may consult the selected works in English translation listed on page 75.

Fey Folk is characteristic of his work. Its characters are quaint, simple-hearted folk living their humble lives in accordance with centuries-old traditions and customs, delightfully described by Papadiamandis with both reverence and humour. The setting is the hinterland of his native isle of Skiathos with its intoxicating vegetation, its hillsides, springs and ravines, where the belief in spirits and the supernatural is deeply rooted in the consciousness of the otherwise God-fearing and devout inhabitants.

David Connolly
Athens, Easter 2013

Fey Folk

That evening, half an hour before the sun went down behind the mountain, Agallos Manouil Agallou had set out to go all the way back to the Arvanitis's, to Manolis's Sorb... no, to Aradias, in the Kechria ravine. The watermill was not so very near... no, nor was it so very far, being less than two hours on foot. But he had dawdled on the way, who knows for what reason. Perhaps he'd been reflecting on his happy, delightful and enviable position of some years before, when he was a handsome and very eligible young man, with endearing eyes and a large red fez, with a long tassel, that he wore cocked to one side. And he had been comparing this with his present

state: a wife who had lost all her freshness and come-
liness and who sat and waited for you at the watermill with two children, one of which told fairytales
to the other. Naturally, this present situation more
than pleased him, but the former seemed exceed-
ingly more desirable and he would willingly have
agreed to begin all over again. Just imagine, eight
years of being betrothed, and to two girls, first to the
one then to the other, sometimes to both at the same
time. If ever in the whole world there was an eligible
young man who lived well, it was him. And old 'ma
Agallaina, God rest her saintly bones wherever they
may be, was more than content. Come Christmas
time, there was the special Christmas loaf* from the
one girl and another loaf from the other. Fried honey
dumplings from the first, turnovers from the second.

---

* *Christmas loaf. St Basil's Cake.* Traditional fare at Christmas and New Year. *Christópsomo* is a round Christmas
loaf decorated with the shape of the cross. *Vassilópitta* is
a cake cut at New Year in honour of St Basil, renowned
for his generosity to the poor. A coin is hidden in the cake
and whoever finds it in his piece will have luck in the
coming year.

Then eight days later, on New Year's Day, St Basil's cake from the one and St Basil's cake from the other. Come Easter again, syrup cake the one, *baklava* the other. Come the feast day of St Agathonicus, *baklava* from Smaragdo, *baklava* from Afendra. And still more syrup cake from Bonoraina, wonderful cook she was, and even more *baklava*. And each time the syrup cake would be bigger in size and the *baklava* twice as thick. But the first girl was unable to get the better of the second. The poor girl was an orphan, all alone in the world: there was no one to look out for her, no one to speak well of her to the in-laws. The other had a more-than-large family, and her brothers, with their lugger, brought her fancy gifts of all kinds. And they put up her dowry and an extra dowry to boot. This is why it was she who won out in the end.

As soon as it grew dark, Afendra lit the lamp, closed her door and, after washing some fresh greens, placed them in a small copper pot, poured water inside, threw some dry wood on the fire and lifted the pot onto the trivet; then she began to blow on the fire. Her two children, seated on the rush matting, were playing: Lenio with her doll, Manolis with his toy boat. The former, a five-year-old, was trying to tell a fairytale to the latter, a four-year-old, who was listening and gaping. She always began with verses:

> *Man's calf for a mother,*
> *A bush for a midwife,*
> *an eagle took me…*

This was about all she knew. But this was enough for Manolis.

Lenio begged her mother to say the rest:

'How does it go, mummy?'

And Afendra continued:

> *An eagle took me,*
> *Lifted me atop a tree.*

'Afterwards, afterwards?' asked Lenio.

'Aterward?' repeated Manolis.

And, in a few words, Afendra related how the maiden born out of a man's calf and with a bush for midwife was loved by a king and then, through the wiles of her mother-in-law, was left by him and condemned to a life tending geese.

And bending over, Afendra blew on the fire, stopping only to say to her children:

'Your father's on his way… he'll be here any time now. Be good children… and he'll have a treat for you… Roasted chickpeas and almonds.'

'Chipeas and amons!' repeated Manolis, his mouth open wide.

The time passed, however, and Agallos was nowhere to be seen. Afendra wasn't concerned, she knew that her husband was a 'slowcoach'. He was like a bride who takes an age to make herself beautiful and, like a bride, walked with a proud air. Ah… a bride! She too had once been a bride… she remembered it still. How could she forget? For eight long years, her mother-in-law had had her dancing to her every tune, and not only her, but the whole of her family as well. Agallos had been a most eligible young man. Eight years, sixteen trays of *baklava*, twenty-four tins of syrup cakes, over forty chickens and pies. And who's to begrudge all that? Yet, so much stubbornness and sulking. Sometimes, he'd break off with the one girl, sometimes with the other. At first, he'd exchanged engagement rings with the other girl. Then they'd fallen out and he'd 'pledged his troth' to her. Afterwards, he'd made up again with the other and gone back on his promise to her. Later, he returned the ring to Smaragdo and got back together again with Afendra. And he was a comely young man, long life to him, and they both loved him. Then again, he was indeed most comely, thought Afendra, fair-skinned, blue-eyed and ruddy-faced. He was even more comely than Afendra herself, who was scrawny, pale and thin. Finally, after he'd taken one last stroll in the direction of Smaragdo's and no one had set eyes on him for a week, the two brothers, who'd arrived with their lugger on the Saturday, got round him, took out the license and married him to Afendra that Sunday evening.

Her kin only just had time to dress the bride. Such finery, such a rich dowry. She herself had embroidered the sun and moon on the sleeves of her scarlet silk chemise. And on her bonnet she had embroidered a large pot with flowers and branches, while on her bodice she had embroidered a variety of sprays. She also had a lovely petticoat made from precious Russian brocade. And the gold embroidered flounce of her skirt was three inches wide.

Her mother-in-law had only just been persuaded at the last minute to give her blessing, having hitherto been adamant, saying that she felt sorry for the other girl, that she pitied her, orphan that she was. Eventually, she donned her best attire and came, wearing her widow's black scarf, keeping the 'fancy' coloured Constantinopolitan scarf to wear only when she would kiss the wedding wreaths.* Her sister-in-law had come too and stood there, beside the

---

* At Greek wedding ceremonies, garlands as well as rings are exchanged between the couple. These are safeguarded in a box and usually kept next to the family icons.

templa, a banked-up pile of bed-furnishings, a living bank herself, tall, broad, unmoving, adorned like a bride. For it doesn't do for the *templa* to be missing from the room where a marriage ceremony is being performed. Mattresses and blankets and rugs carefully folded, pillows and sheets piled orderly and neatly against the wall in one corner of the room, covered by a silk sheet and crowned with two silk-covered bolsters: such is the *templa*.*

Once the best man had arrived with the fiddlers, then the guests came, followed by the priests, and the ceremony began. The rings were exchanged, then the wedding wreaths, the wonderful blessings were read out and the wedding hymn 'Rejoice Isaiah' sung. In keeping with the custom, the newlyweds walked three times in a circle and were showered with rice and sugared almonds. Finally, reaching out his hard and bony hand, Father Nikolas took hold of an eight-year old boy who had both his father and mother, shoved him between the

---

* A custom peculiar to the author's native island of Skiathos.

newlyweds and, separating their joined hands with the boy's head, loudly wished them 'may all your children be male'.

Next, taking up the large tray, the groom himself offered sweetmeats to the priests, the best man and the guests, while the bride, standing erect between the *templa* and her sister-in-law, looked on in pride, and it required the bridesmaids, all decked out and standing in attendance, to gently rock her head from behind to make her nod in response to the plethora of wishes from the guests: 'Long life to you both! May you be blessed with sons!' while her lips barely moved to say thank you and her voice was inaudible.

In the meantime, *Barba*-Ghioulis,* the cook hired for all the weddings, had lit two large fires in the front yard of the house. On one he placed a huge cauldron used for distilling *raki*, into which he cut up an eight-month-old lamb and began browning

---

* *Bárba* literally means uncle, but the word is attached as a prefix to the first names of elderly men to show respect and intimacy.

it to make the Persian pilaf customarily served at weddings, while over the other fire, once the charcoal was ready, he placed two spits side by side with two more slaughtered lambs.

Leaning over the two fires, he turned the spit with his one hand and in the other he held the huge ladle with which he stirred and browned the meat and onions. Ol' Sigourantsas, a self-invited assistant, also came to turn the other spit. As soon as the meat began to brown, as soon as the pot roast began to emit a mouth-watering aroma, Ghioulis, taking out the knife from his wide, yellow sash, began cutting generous morsels from the two roasts and, using the ladle, scooped out some big pieces from the pot roast. He gulped down three pieces, as an appetizer, so he said, and gave one to ol' Sigourantsas to satisfy his craving, and on seeing two or three 'hangers-on', whom the old-timers called 'recorders' and who apparently keep a precise register with the exact dates of births, marriages and saints' name-days, he began to drive them away with reproaches and threats, rather like a house-cat that, discovering all its tigerish nature and bristling its fur and snarling threateningly, suddenly scratches at the eyes of the good-natured raiding dog as it instinctively approaches.

On hearing Ghioulis's gruff voice from above as he was driving away the pestering cadgers, one of the guests (who had himself just previously turned them out of the house, after having treated them several times to *baklava* together with mastic and rum), stuck his head out of the window and saw Ghioulis, who was a professed enemy of *baklava* and all confectionery, generously slicing into the loin of the roasting lamb with his broad knife. Whereupon, the guest not only did not reprove him, but feeling his own appetite whetted, secretly took hold of one of the many jugs filled with wine that the guests had brought, and quietly coming down into the yard, offered it to Ghioulis, who gulped down a goodly measure and gratefully cutting off a large morsel offered it to the discreet fellow. After two or three reciprocal courtesies of this kind, the jug was half-empty.

The two roasts were eventually cooked and the pilaf too. Then, Ghioulis removed the huge cauldron from the fire and also put the two spits to one side. And after he'd stirred and stirred the rice and swallowed two or three spoonfuls to try it, he began emptying the rice into deep serving dishes, and carving the two roasts into large pieces, continuing as he did so to taste it all, not once but twice. But it was time to take the brimming dishes up into the house and the guests arranged themselves in long lines along the length and breadth of the large room and ate and made merry in honour of the newly-weds.

Then the various jugs and bottles began to go round in different directions through the ranks of the revellers. *Barba*-Konstandis Xesouros, the bride's uncle, holding in his left hand a large ten-litre demijohn which he rested on his knee and in his right a small fifty-dram glass, poured the wine for the guests, courteously pouring one glass for the first person on his right, then modestly drinking one himself, then pouring one for the person on his left, and having one himself so as to drink the health of both, or offering a glass to the second person on his right, and downing one himself to return the good wishes, and so on and so forth. There was great merriment and the floor almost gave way beneath the dancing. The festivities lasted a whole week. It was a wedding, said Afendra, that would long be remembered in the village.

It had been dark for over an hour, and the flickering lamp lit the sparse room separated off inside the mill, and the fire glowed comfortingly in the corner, and the fresh wild cabbage, which Afendra had cut with her own hand, gathering it with not a little toil from the ravine's snow-covered slopes, from among the rocks and bushes surrounding the ramshackle watermill beside the old plane trees, had now boiled.

But Agallos hadn't arrived and Lenio was still reciting the fairytale to her brother. She'd already repeated the first verses of the song at least ten times; verses summarizing the beautiful girl's bizarre adventure in the fairytale, and still she hadn't learned them. She'd now come to the final verses.

An old woman tricked me,
in the king's arms.

And she called for help to her mother, who completed the song as follows:

in the king's arms;
the king with his mother,
while I tend the geese.

And before learning them herself, Lenio took it upon her to teach the verses to Manolis who, spluttering, repeated them:

An ol' woman ticked me
in the kling's arms.

Suddenly, a loud banging was heard. Someone was outside knocking on the door, which Afendra had bolted from the inside as she was accustomed to doing when she was alone at the watermill with her children. In delight, Afendra leapt up, took the lamp, descended the four wooden steps which led down from the room to the mill floor, and went to open the front door. The children ran behind her, jumping up and down.

Before she had even opened the door, Afendra heard a woman's enquiring voice outside:

'What have you locked yourselves in for? My, my, it's not night yet.'

It wasn't Agallos. Afendra recognised the voice: it was her mother.

The old woman came in carrying a basket on her arm, with her black outer-skirt laid under the handle of the basket, wearing only her old faded dress, her woollen stockings with holes in the toes and heels and without shoes. The children immediately rushed towards the basket, and looked to see what was concealed inside beneath the folded outer-skirt, hoping that their granny had brought a treat for them from the village, but all they found was the aged woman's old clogs, which she always carried in the basket, preferring to walk barefoot so that her feet might be free but also in order to preserve her clogs.

Seeing her mother entering instead of her husband, Afendra supposed that the latter must have stayed behind to spend the night in the village, as he sometimes did, and so she wasn't too surprised. But when they got up to the room, ol' Synodia, seeing that Agallos wasn't there, asked:

'Where's your husband?'

Afendra stared at her in bewilderment.

'Didn't you leave him in the village?'

'No; he set off an hour before me.'

'To come here?'

'Yes, here.'

'And why hasn't he arrived then?'

'Why hasn't he arrived?'

'Where is he?

'Where is he, indeed!'

The two women were overcome with great anxiety. Afendra wrung her hands in distress.

'Whatever can have befallen him?'

'Where can he be?'

'Why didn't you come together since you were going to come yourself?' asked Afendra, complainingly.

'It wasn't sure. I had things to do. I was in two minds about whether to come. You go on, I told him, before night falls, and I'll see. I'm used to walking in the ravines at night.'

And, indeed, they were all accustomed to trudging at night through the hills and dales. The two mothers-in-law, 'ma Synodia and Agallos's mother, may she rest in peace, had two watermills in the Kechria ravine. The mill belonging to Agallos's family had been in disuse for some time and was deserted now. But the mill belonging to Synodia, widowed of late, was still in operation. And because he was used to having a mill, Agallos demanded the mill as part of his dowry, and 'ma Synodia was forced to let him have it. Both families, parents and forebears, had been partly brought up in the village, where they had cottages, and partly in the Kechria ravine, where they had their mills. Women and men, sons and daughters, were not afraid of walking in the wood at night.

They were regarded as rather 'fey' folk, though they weren't afraid of spirits. It's true that they themselves often recounted how they'd seen sprites and the like, but they spoke with a courteous tongue about ghosts. They were neither harassed nor harmed by them. They were on good terms with them. Agallos often recounted how he'd seen fairies with his own eyes, how they'd spoken to him and how he'd made sure not to answer them, aware that they had the power to 'rob him of his speech'. Then again, when he was still a boy at his father's mill, his fairy godmother had appeared to him and had given him a florin with her own hand. He was certain of it, and still had the florin and showed it. So that no one might think he was a fraud or that he didn't believe it himself. On the contrary. He believed it with all his being.

Yet compared with 'ma Synodia, there was no one who knew more when it came to sprites and the like. From birth, she'd been on the friendliest of terms with the fairies. She knew the sprites, the blackamoors with their long pipes, the Lamias and the hobgoblins that would be coming then at Christmastide. The house spirit never does any harm. Sometimes it appears as a peaceful lamb, sometimes as a broody hen with its chickens. Fairies like to come out during daylight, when it's warm, and dance in the midday sun.

Don't let them trick you and make you open your mouth to speak to them, because they'll take away your speech and you'll remain dumb. The blackamoor with his long pipe and the Turkish she-devil with her veil come out at night and sit around the springs in the ravines. The hobgoblins like to scare people, to hide inside chimneys and play nasty pranks. Apart from this, they're harmless. Only the vampire is evil, Lord preserve us. Yet it seeks only its own kin.

'Ma Synodia was certain that her son-in-law couldn't have come to any harm from the hob-goblins, who would only just now be on their way there as it was Christmas Eve. Besides, Agallos was a Saturday-child, and it's well-known that whoever has this good fortune is not subject to the wiles of spirits.* Nevertheless, she couldn't understand why her son-in-law was so late, as he'd set off from the village an hour before her, and she'd come by the same path that they always took.

'The one we always come by, dear child,' she said to her daughter, 'Where could he have got to? What can have happened?'

'Could he have been drinking and fallen somewhere because of the snow?'

'He didn't seem at all drunk, dear child; and what snow are you talking of? The path's clear all the way… just a bit of trodden snow here and there… the only place where there's any snow to talk of is up on the heights. And when have you ever seen real snow? You should have seen it in my old granddad's days, when I was a little girl, as high as two men the snow was, three men… It blocked the door so we

---

* In Greek folklore, the child born on Saturday is especially blessed and has supernatural powers, which include the ability to communicate with spirits.

couldn't get out, right up to the lintel, two yards deep it was. While we were clearing the snow from in front of the door, and we were at it with spades and shovels for two hours, the roof that was creaking under the snow suddenly fell, crack! and flattened us.'

The two children, who had lost their jollity and were now almost in tears, involuntarily raised their eyes to the ceiling that the old woman had pointed to while recounting her story.

'Mummy! What's granny saying?' shouted Lenio, bursting into tears. 'Daddy's been flattened by the snow… and the roof is going to fall and flatten us too!'

'Hush, hush! Don't cry child,' Afendra cried out. 'Granny was just talking… don't be afraid… daddy will be along any moment and he's sure to have some sweets for you…'

'Hush, darling Lenio,' said the old woman. 'I've come on purpose to get you up early in the morning, to take you to St Elijah's, so you can receive communion, my dear little girl…'

'And me, and me!' cried Manolis.

'And you too, young lad…'

'Is there going to be a service tomorrow at St Elijah's?' Afendra asked, momentarily forgetting her worry.

'Yes there is… and at long last; it's about time you had a little incense over you… Get ready, young lady, get your things on quickly and let's be off… Your husband must have turned off along the way and gone to some cottage to find a friend… perhaps he went to buy some *mizithra* cheese* or fresh cream for tomorrow… Don't worry… Wherever he is, he'll turn up.

So, indeed, on learning that Father Konstandis Brikolas would come up the hill in the morning to celebrate the liturgy at the country church of the Prophet Elijah at the request of some shepherds and farmers, the old woman had decided to go to the Kechria ravine rather than spend Christmas in the village and persuade her daughter and grandchildren to get up early in the morning and go up

---

* Soft, unsalted white cheese.

to the church, which was situated half way along the path, on a level clearing close to the top of the hill, an hour from the village and an hour from Kechria, in order to attend the service and take communion, so that she might make humans of them, as she said, as they'd been down in the ravine for months without going to church.

It was very rare for a priest to come and celebrate the liturgy in the tiny church at Kechria, which was an old, ruined monastery, annexed as a dependency of the cenobitic Monastery of the Annunciation, and if a priest did come, Agallos, Afendra and their two children, dwelling as they did in the ravine and having the stumbling gait of river crabs, would be unlikely to hear of it so as to go and attend the service. Since Agallos had sold his family house in the village and had been permanently living at the mill, he went to church only once a year, on 23rd August, on the ninth day after the Dormition of the Holy Virgin when the tiny church in Kechria celebrated its feast day.

Finally, ol' Synodia put her hand deep inside her dress and took it out full of almonds and hazelnuts, which she divided between the two children. She unfolded her new black outer-skirt in which to their great surprise there was a small sweet-smelling Christmas cake wrapped in a cloth that she handed to her daughter, saying: 'Compliments of the season!'

Afendra emptied some of the greens on to a plate and sat the two children down to eat, certain that if they ate, they'd go straight to sleep and thus 'they wouldn't be a nuisance and they'd be able to wake up early the next morning.'

After eating the almonds that his granny had given him and then swallowing a couple of mouth-fuls of greens, Manolis was the first to shut his eyes and fall asleep in his chair. His mother laid him down beside the hearth on a wool rug and covered him with one end of the quilt. She made the sign of the cross three times over his head and left him to sleep.

Lenio didn't want to go to bed, saying that she wanted to wait up for her father, who had promised to bring her a pretty trinket from the village. But 'ma Synodia put her on her knee, covered her with her old dress to keep her warm and rocked her so much that she made her sleepy. Before long, she'd fallen asleep, and her mother, lifting her from the old woman's lap, cradling her in her arms and lulling her with 'coo… coo…', laid her next to Manolis.

Agallos had still not arrived and the two women, who were becoming increasingly anxious as the night progressed, now free of any annoyance from the children, discussed what should be done. The old woman said that if, God forbid, her son-in-law had fallen anywhere on the way, she would have seen him as she had come by the same path that they always took. Except, she was forced to admit, somewhat belatedly, when she'd reached Kechria, she hadn't passed by the little Monastery of the Holy Virgin.

'Why?' her daughter asked.

'I passed lower down there, by the olive grove.'

A little north of the Holy Virgin's of Kechria was one of Synodia's olive groves. Before arriving at the Holy Virgin's, she had turned off and gone to have a look at the olive grove, even though night had fallen. She was afraid that the snowfall of five days previously might have broken some of the olive trees' branches and she went there to see for herself, even though it was night. On arriving there, she saw that no damage had been done by the snow and, now content, she returned to the path lower down by way of the ravine, and arrived at the mill without passing by the Holy Virgin's of Kechria.

'So, let's go there and take a look,' suggested Afendra hesitantly, who apparently with this in mind had hurried to put the children to bed.

'It wouldn't be wise for you to come' said Synodia. The children will wake up and see that they're alone; they won't know what to do and they'll be scared out of their wits.'

'What can we do?' asked Afendra.

'I'll go and look on my own in case he's fallen anywhere… He might have gone inside the church to light a candle before the icons.'

'How can you go off all alone again?'

'I'll take the oil cruse to light the lamps in the

Holy Virgin's… I've brought candles with me from the village… Don't worry!'

'Where can that man have got to! I'll go crazy. I'm almost at my wits' end!' cried Afendra, straining even more, as women do, through their spontaneous but uncontrolled emotions, her already strained nerves.

At that same moment, they heard the sound of a high-pitched voice in song:

Twee, twee, my peacock, twee, twee!
Come here, come here to my knee…

'Oh, it's Peacock!' said ol' Synodia. Hold on, we'll call him.'

And without waiting for her daughter to speak, ol' Synodia went down to the ground floor, opened the front door of the mill and began shouting loudly.

'Peacock! Hey, Peacock!'

The singer, astride his donkey, was passing by the mill, on the other side of the ravine, travelling along a path leading from the Aradias wood to the Kechria seashore.

He wasn't visible among the trees in the darkness. But they could hear the donkey's clopping, the switch hitting against its rump and the cry of its rider 'Gee up, get on there!', which he directed at the beast whenever he left off from his favourite song, which had given him his nick-name: the one 'ma Synodia had used to call out to him.

He was apprenticed to a landowner who lived in the town, and he tended his master's cattle below St Eleni's, where the latter had extensive pastures and a small cottage. He must have been delayed in town, for some reason, so it seemed, and he was returning late to the cottage, which was not a rare occurrence.

'Peacock! Hey, Peacock!'

'What is it, 'ma Synodia?' replied the young farmhand, recognizing her voice.

'Are you coming directly from the village, or not?'

'From the village, by way of St Yannakis's, Synodaris, Vromovryssi, Philippeika, the Mamou gully, Vigles, Stamelou, Petralono…'

'Have you passed by all those places, Peacock?'

'All of them and still more...'

'Have you seen my son-in-law, Agallos, any-where?'

'Your son-in-law, Agallos?... Why, hasn't he arrived? He'll have bumped into his fairy godmother again... Perhaps she came to him in a dream and got him to go and find some *groschen*, and told him to go at night time so no one would see him... Or he'll have bumped into some spirits on the way and got into conversation with them and forgot the time...'

'Enough of the twaddle, because we're sick with worry, lad... Don't make light of it... Who knows what's happened to him... Do me a favour, dear Peacock, will you come up with me, as far as the Holy Virgin's, to see if we can find him anywhere?'

'Let's go, what have we to lose?' said the young lad, willingly.

And turning his beast towards the stream's chan-nel, he came to a place where he knew that the stream narrowed to only two spans in width and spurred on his donkey, which had halted, not wanting to step into the water and cross the stream and so he arrived in front of the mill.

Having been persuaded to stay with her children in the mill, Afendra lit a small lamp and put the bottle of oil and three candles in a basket. This time, 'ma Synodia wore her black outer-skirt, put on her clogs and, taking hold of the basket and the lamp, followed Peacock, who had dismounted, tied his donkey to a tree and had set off on foot.

Peacock walked ahead in silence because, on seeing the woman's worry regarding her husband's fate, he had felt sorrow and respect and had of his own accord ceased his merry song.

'Ma Synodia followed behind, walking slowly along the wet narrow path, where not long before the snow had been trodden down and had hardened, forming a thin layer as far as the low vale in the west which lay next to the sea. Instinctively, she looked to left and right, through the branches that formed a cool green border along the uphill path, with an inner fear, afraid of suddenly seeing the body of her son-in-law lying between a clump of gorse and an arbutus bush. For she was extremely worried and had no idea what might have happened to the ne'er-do-well. Every so often, a branch would fall from above with a crack and a thud, breaking off the tree with a shower of snow, which coolly caressed the eyes and brows of the two nocturnal wayfarers. Coming from the left through the branches and bushes, a last weak gust of the North Wind, visiting in those lower regions his virgin sister, the snow, turned the infinitely varied patterns that she had so majestically spread over the boughs of the trees into crystal. It was not without reason that Proteus, the figure from ancient mythology, was so-called. In an allegorical way, the creative mind of that most gifted of all peoples wished to show that one primary seed, embedded in the world by the Creator and procreating in infinite combinations, would produce such an infinite variety of individual types and forms that no two leaves are alike, as that truest of sayings goes.

To the right, on the other side of the ravine, began the Aradias Wood, consisting of thousand-year-old oaks climbing all the way up the mountain to its highest point at St Constantine's, and the mountain, tall and sheer, appeared like a vast ivy-covered wall. Snow shone here and there on the face of the dark forest, a white mystery, silent, responding in the language of the stars to the Pleiades above, to the North Star, to the Bear and the entire galaxy. And through the gusts of the North Wind, which blew through the leaves of the age-old trees, the forest – magnificent, haunted, unsullied, unravaged by fire and, as was said, inflicting harm on any woodcutter who dared to raise an irreverent axe against it – related in a language incomprehensible to all how many eras and ages it had lived through, and how many generations of men it had seen, one after the other, but without the later ones learning from the experience of the earlier and becoming wiser. And the frosty wind of the forest, chill, icy, plaintive, rippling through trees and crevices, reached across to the other milder side and transmitted its chill to the shoulders and backs of the two nocturnal wayfarers.

They had already reached the first high ground, from where the olive groves began to spread out to the left of them. Suddenly Peacock, perhaps because he felt cold and wished to get warm, perhaps trying to comfort 'ma Synodia, who he could see was downcast and worried about her son-in-law, started up once again singing his favourite song:

Twee, twee, my peacock, twee, twee!
Come here, come here to my knee…

'Ma Synodia, who had remained for a few moments staring at the east slope, cut him short:

'Over there,' she said to him, 'what's that?'

She pointed to the dome of the little church of the Holy Virgin of Kechria, which rose above the walls of the church and the monastery and became visible behind the trees in a sudden flash of light. Behind the monastery's west wall, which was lower, plain and without cells, sparks rose into the sky, lighting the dome and the western side of the church's roof, as if there was a fire burning in the church grounds.

'Ma Synodia crossed herself and let out a sigh.

'Holy Mother of God!'

'What can it be?' said Peacock, obliged to cut short his song for a second time.

'Didn't you pass by the church earlier, on your way here?'

'No!'

'Me neither. Shall we go and see?'

'Let's go!'

Afendra waited at the watermill, huddled up by the hearth and beside the sleeping children. There was no longer any sound of fairytales or songs in the silent mill; her mother wasn't present to comfort her by way of her cheerful and vigorous old age, and those reminiscences of her wedding, momentarily recalled, had gone, not wishing to implant themselves in a grieving spirit and a sad home. The only sounds to be heard and her sole company were the breathing of the sleeping children and the crackling of the fire occasionally emitted by the glowing logs, and her gaze remained intentionally fixed on the lamp burning before the icon of the Three Holy Figures that she had received as her dowry, depicting Christ in the middle, standing erect, blessing with his right hand and holding a book in his left, with his gentle expression, his beauteous form, his slightly parted fair beard, his blue raiment and red seamless robe. To Christ's right was the Holy Mother of God, to his left St John the Baptist, both bowing with arms crossed at either side of the Lord. And next to the icon, hanging from a nail and wrapped in a piece of white veil, were the two wedding wreaths. Ah, yes, the recollections from the wedding were still coming, but unpleasant ones and in another guise.

For more than once since then her mother had told her that she was afraid of the spells that might be cast on her by the other, her rival, the orphan girl unjustly passed over. It wasn't the spirits that she was afraid of, even though she was said to be fey, or rather she was so called precisely because of this, because, whatever she saw, she was never afraid. But when it came to spells, this was another matter. First of all, she was afraid lest her rival 'fill her with girls', a goal that is achieved through certain incantations made while the prayers for the betrothal are being read, immediately before the main wedding ceremony. Her fear increased initially when her daughter's first-born was a girl, but eased when her second was a son. 'The spells didn't work,' she said. Next, seeing that her 'ne'er-do-well' son-in-law was not doing very well in his business affairs, that he'd been forced to sell his family house and become a country bumpkin, she declared 'you're not going to prosper, daughter'. It was only to be expected. It's no small matter, stealing away the orphan girl's good fortune to get married yourself. But then again what are you to do? How else can you live? Life's like that; it's war. To attain perfection, to put the other before yourself… it's like deciding not to live in this world. It's like going and drowning yourself. Just thinking about it clouds your wits. It's enough to send you out into the wilderness.

Yet was this then the greatest evil, which sometimes happening unavoidably, brings implacable
hatred between two families? There were others far
worse. The smaller the village, the bigger the evil.
Hatred ran amok and in so doing prevailed between
families and individuals. It ran through all the arter-
ies and through all the veins of a small community.
The sacred law of Christ was transgressed, evil was
always returned for evil, multiple evil for good,
never good for evil. An insurmountable wall separated the two parties, the two factions. You'd think
they lived together in order to hate each other, that
fate made them residents of that same township in
order to quarrel with each other. Every leading man
in his time, whether it was the mayor or local deputy
or whatever he was called, implemented in full the
popular saying: 'first take care of your own'. He was
the protector of his family, his kin, his friends, his
party, not the protector of the township. And in
addition to this basic division, there were hundreds
of other sub-divisions. The one neighbourhood
declared war on the other neighbourhood; each

family on the other families; each individual on the other individuals. The one neighbour didn't so much as say good morning to the other, let alone a kind word. Each rejoiced at seeing the other's misfortune. When it was a question of some inheritance, the relatives argued as to who would get the most. They would rather go to court, be sold as slaves in Barbary, than see their relative get more than them. For a quarter of an acre of land, they were quite capable of getting into all sorts of disputes, of driving themselves to death with 'temporary measures', 'legal proceedings', 'appeals' and 'counter appeals'. If some unfortunate olive tree happened to have one of its branches hanging slightly over the adjacent field, the neighbour would rush with his spade in the night to re-dig the borders and shift the boundary ditch. The next day, the astonished olive tree would wake to find itself in the neighbour's grove. It had changed owner during the night.

Whole battles were fought for a newly-grafted tree in an olive grove, for three vines of a vineyard, for half a stretch of wheat field. And the olive-trees had for seven long years ceased to bear fruit, as if deeming the heads of these sinners unworthy to be anointed with their oil; and the vines, prematurely turning pale, did not provide ripe wine-bearing bunches, refusing to delight the hearts of unworthy people with their ambrosial juice; and the golden wheat of the earth prematurely bowed its withered head to its mother, desiring to quickly return to her bosom, not wishing to nourish the bellies of irreverent people.

Such were the wars that the men waged against each other, and such were their spoils. But were the women any less belligerent?

The mother didn't want her daughter's good, the mother-in-law deeply hated her daughter-in-law. The daughter-in-law didn't so much as say good morning to her sister-in-law.

For the sake of an unguarded word, for the slightest backbiting, which found many gossips willing to convey what had been said, usually enlarged out of all proportion, to the person concerned, they were quite capable of not speaking to each other for the rest of their lives. 'Wouldn't lay my bones in the same grave as yours!' was the battle cry in the women's ranks. One night, 'ma Synodia had had a terrifying dream, which would have been a true vision if she hadn't had it previously in her mind. She was dozing lightly one evening, mumbling to herself these very words, hurled at her that same day by a female relative and enemy of hers, 'Wouldn't lay my bones in the same grave as yours!' She fell asleep and recalled the cemetery, the ossuary in the town's old graveyard, close to which she often passed as she returned in the evening from the fields, and in which she saw the white and yellowed bones of the dead all mixed up, all lying together, without it being possible to discern with the eye which were the bones of old friends and which were those of enemies. While she was dozing, she dreamt that she was passing by the cemetery and heard a terrible din made by hard objects clashing together. She looked up and saw the bones of the dead standing on end, moving, shaking and striking each other. Ulna clashed with ulna, forearm with forearm, fibula with fibula, rib with rib, backbone with backbone. Two bare skulls that had been discarded there, perhaps because they were unworthy to be respectfully exhumed after three years and given a memorial service, were pulverized by the hail of blows that they received from the furious tibias. On seeing this strange spectacle, 'ma Synodia attempted to cross herself and whispered: '*Kyrie eleison!*' Who wouldn't be shocked, even though asleep? Imagine seeing the bones in the cemetery come alive, rise up and begin striking each other and making such a fearful noise!* In the end, while still terrified at the sight and wondering what would happen, she heard a loud crack and an even bigger din and saw one of the walls of the cemetery, the north one, which was higher than the others, suddenly collapse inwards, falling on all the bones and shattering them. 'Ma

---

* The author is not claiming the creation of this device, presented here purely for didactical reasons, since it may have originated from the unconscious recollection of previous readings. [Author's note]

Synodia gleefully thought 'serves them right!' and woke up.

She wanted to relate this vision, that she'd had only a few days previously, to her confessor, but she hadn't found the time to go on Christmas Eve. She hoped she'd have time the next morning at St Elijah's, where she intended to go to confess and unburden her conscience. But coming to the mill, she saw that her son-in-law was missing and she simply couldn't account for his strange delay. Now she'd left her daughter waiting with her sleeping children in the mill and together with Peacock, sent by a beneficient providence to help her, 'was sailing' through the night, albeit on land, above the ravine towards the Holy Virgin's. And Afendra too, reflecting in her solitude, seated opposite the lovely icon of the Three Holy Figures, felt the need to unburden her conscience. Prior to her marriage, she had lent an ear to old wives' tales about spells and potions for ensnaring a groom and, for a while, she had hoped through powders and philtres to steal the heart of her fiancé from the orphan girl, her rival, and win it for herself. And for seven long years she'd resolved a hundred times to do it but not once had she found the courage to confess this sin.

It was already after midnight, deep into the night, and from that profound silence, from those barely audible noises, so faint that it was impossible to tell whether they were the product of hearing or imagination, that vague and mysterious and inexplicable enchantment, Afendra, though not at all sleepy, felt that the hour was late. A long December night, *endless night*. Suddenly she heard the first cockcrow. The cock, who with seven hens, was housed in a small coop behind the millstone and the flour chute, like a pasha with his harem, had sensed the hour and let out his usual cry. Afendra, who had already begun to doze, without having lain down, suddenly awoke.

'The cock's crowing,' she murmured, 'it's past midnight… what can have happened to my mother?'

Her mother's delay bode no good. Yet, paradoxically, her hopes were raised and she was certain that no evil had befallen them.

She got up and poked the fire. Taking hold of the lamp, she went downstairs to get some dry wood and, coming back, threw it on the fire. Then she crossed herself three times before the holy icon and said the 'Our Father' and 'the Creed', the only prayers she knew.

At that same moment, the sound of a man's footsteps was heard outside. There was a banging on her door. It was Peacock's voice. She rushed to let him in.

Dawdling like a bride, Agallos slowly descended the hillside before arriving at Kechria, and though it was already dark, he persisted in his memories of those happy years when he was a prized catch, envied and sought after, and had enjoyed himself for eight whole years betrothed to two girls, first dallying with the one and then with the other. But when he arrived before the old monastery of the Holy Virgin of Kechria, he turned leftwards to face the church and make the sign of the cross and, through the open gate of the church grounds, saw a bright light inside the church. Some pious woman must have remembered to light the Holy Virgin's lamps on the eve of her immaculate Childbirth and must have overdone it with the oil and wicks, turning the lamps into brands. But at the same time, he heard voices and whispering inside the church, like the readings or quiet chanting of monks in prayer. Who could it be? The monastery had been in disuse since the time of the Regency; the church had remained deserted.

Agallos may have been fey, but he was also a Saturday-child and was not afraid. He walked up to the monastery gate, entered the enclosure, walked across the grounds and went into the church. The lamps were lit in front of the icons on the screen, but with a normal flame and not like fire-brands. But there were also two large candles burning in the candelabrum together with five or six smaller ones. This was the source of the bright light.

To the right in the apse, a middle-aged monk wearing the long veiled headdress of an archimandrite was chanting the hymn, 'Lord, I called upon

Thee'. It was daybreak on Monday and vespers hadn't been sung that morning nor had the liturgy of St Basil the Great been celebrated on the previous evening.* To the left, another monk was responding antiphonically to the first. Two or three other monks or novices, wearing cassocks though without the headdresses, were standing on the west side of the church in the stalls. From within the sanctuary at that moment, wearing a stole, a chasuble and holding a censor, emerged a reverend elder, a hieromonk, tall, bony, hoary, bearded and with pale, lean and almost transparent features. Who were they all? It was the first time Agallos had ever set eyes on them.

The venerable presbyter first censed the icons, then the cantor on the right, then the one on the left, next the three monks or novices and, last of all, Agallos. Agallos bowed in the direction of the censor and seeing the lean and transparent features of the venerable priest was convinced that he'd gone, while still alive, to Paradise. There was no other way he could explain this vision.

Not one of the five monks turned to look at the newcomer. Only the last one, the youngest of those wearing robes, who wasn't wearing a headdress, but was holding his folded black cap under his arm, without looking, turned the side of his head with his mane of hair, and, without looking, the corner of his eye to Agallos. So, Agallos plucked up the courage to go over to him and ask:

'Who are you all?'

The novice gestured by way of reply that it wasn't a time for explanations, but the venerable priest, who had returned to the sanctuary and seemingly having the gift of foresight, turned to the novice and by way of a nod gave him his permission to provide their brother with an explanation.

When Agallos had satisfied his curiosity, he made up his mind to leave and go down to the mill and bring his wife and children all together up to the Church of the Holy Virgin, because the strange monks were going to keep an all-night vigil and celebrate the liturgy towards daybreak. But as he was about to leave, he thought again to himself: 'I'll stay a bit longer' and then 'a bit longer' and it was already approaching midnight without him having felt at all tired. For he found the sweetness and decorum of the chanting most pleasing.

Finally, just before midnight, when they had begun reading the Synaxarion* of the day and just as Agallos had turned to go outside to warm himself a little next to the blazing fire and was thinking of his wife's anxiety, as he was sure that his mother-in-law would have already arrived from the village and told Afendra of his departure from the town, he suddenly saw his mother-in-law and Peacock before him.

Agallos didn't allow ol' Synodia's fey nature to begin to work. He called to her to come outside the church and told her who these monks were.

It was decided that Peacock, who in any case had left his donkey tied up outside the mill, should be

---

* Read during matins, it relates the main events of the lives of the saints and martyrs commemorated on that day and, on major feasts, the main events of that feast.

sent to give a simple message to Afendra telling her that in two hours' time, her husband and mother would come down to wake the two children and bring them and their mother to the Holy Virgin's to attend the liturgy.

Afendra rushed and opened the door.

'Are you alone? Where's my mother?'

'At the Holy Virgin's.'

'The Holy Virgin's? And Agallos?'

'Agallos too. They're attending the vigil.'

'Vigil?'

'Yes, an all-night vigil.'

'Who's celebrating it?'

'Some newly-arrived monks.'

'Monks?'

'Yes, men in cassocks.'

'Are they from the monastery?'

'No, they're from elsewhere. They've just arrived. They're staying at St Thanasis's.'

'St Thanasis's?'

'Yes. That's all I know. They said you should get some sleep and before long Agallos will come with 'ma Synodia to wake you, to get the children and take you to receive communion. Good night and may tomorrow bring you good fortune.'

Afendra only just managed to steal a nap before there was a knocking on the door of the watermill. It was Agallos and 'ma Synodia.

Afendra woke the children, washed them, clothed them, combed their hair, adorned herself with whatever she had to hand in the mill and, taking the lamp, the five of them set out for the Holy Virgin's.

The six monks were indeed newly-arrived. They had come from one of the Cycladic isles, where they had lived as ascetics for many years. They had arrived just a few weeks previously and most of the inhabitants still didn't know about them. It was the first time that Agallos had seen them, which is why he'd taken them for a strange vision. On arriving, they had begun to build cells to live in, temporarily housing themselves in a village hut.

Since there was no church in those parts, they had come down to celebrate Christmas at Kechria, an hour's walk away.

Some called them heretics, others again respected them as being most virtuous men. It was commonly said that they had in part embraced the doctrines of a religious teacher which had been denounced by the Holy Synod. The truth was that it was this teacher who had followed the old customs of a very archaic monastic community, to which these ascetics belonged. Thus they coincided in part in their doctrines. There are many, however, who believe that, since the majority of people thirst for religious instruction and those responsible and competent do little to meet this need by drawing on pure and orthodox sources rather than foreign and distorted ones, it was only to be expected that many pious and well-intentioned people would be misled, in good faith, on hearing the Christian doctrine, albeit adulterated, wherever this is preached, because when the springs and fountains grow cloudy, with those in authority concealing the clear spring waters, men and beasts, dying of thirst, will prefer to drink from the cloudy stream, finding some slight hope of deliverance in this, rather than die of thirst; *O Lord, thou preservest man and beast. How excellent is thy loving kindness, O God!**

'Ma Synodia confessed to Father Ezekiel (as the abbot of the brotherhood was called) and he counselled her that if the orphan girl, who had been passed over as a result of her daughter's marriage, was still unmarried, she must, in order to find forgiveness, do everything in her power to get her settled; if, however, the girl had married or died meanwhile, then she would have to perform other forms of good works, as well as attending Forty Liturgies, preferably at her parish church.

---

* Psalm 36 : 6-7.

Since Synodia informed him that the girl was still unmarried, the first directive was imposed on her.

Afendra, who at last found the courage to confess her sin of spellbinding, was required for her penance to abstain from receiving Holy Communion for a long period and, in addition, to fast and pray. She was advised to light a large candle to St Anastasia, the maker of healing unguents.

The two children received Holy Communion, and the family returned together to their mill as the sun was rising.

Biographical Note

1851   (4 March) Born in Skiathos.

1856-60 Primary School in Skiathos.

1866-67 Begins his secondary education in Skiathos.

1867-70 High School in Chalkis (Euboea).

1872   Visits Mount Athos.

1873-74 Graduates from High School in Athens.

1874-75 Enrols in the School of Philosophy at the
University of Athens.

1877   Military service.

1879   Publication of his first literary work,
Η μετανάστις (The Migrant), in the Greek-
language newspaper *Neologos* in Istanbul.

1880-81   Recalled to the army to complete his
          military service.

1881   Literary debut in Athens with his poem
          "Δέηση" (Supplication) in the Athenian
          newspaper *Soter*.

1882   Works as a translator for the newspaper
          Ephemeris. Publication of his novel *Οι
          έμποροι των εθνών* (The Traders in Nations)
          under the pseudonym "Bohème".

1884   Publication under his real name of his work
          Η γυφτοπούλα (The Gypsy Girl) in the news-
          paper *Acropolis*.

1887   Begins going to the church of Aghios
          Elissaios in Monastiraki (Athens). Writes
          his first short story, *Το Χριστόψωμο*
          (The Christmas Loaf).

1888-91   Regular contributor to the newspaper
          Ephemeris.

1892-97   Works on a regular basis as both editor and
          translator for the newspaper *Acropolis*.

1896   Publication of his short story *Ο έρωτας στα
          χιόνια* (Love in the Snow).

1898   Works as a translator for the newspaper
          Asty.

1900   Publication of his short story Όνειρο στο
        κύμα (Dream on the Wave).

1902   Publication of a collection of his short
        stories. Returns to Skiathos, where he
        remains until 1904.

1904   Lives in Athens. Publication of his work
        Η φόνισσα (The Murderess) in the
        newspaper *Panathenaea*.

1908   Returns to Skiathos.

1910   Falls gravely ill.

1911   Dies in Skiathos, his birthplace, on 3rd
        January.

Selected Works
in English Translation

Papadiamandis, Alexandros, *The Murderess: A Social Tale*, trans. Liadain Sherrard, eds Lampros Kamperidis, Denise Harvey, Limni, Evia: Denise Harvey, 2011.

Papadiamandis, Alexandros, *The Boundless Garden: Selected Short Stories*, trans. David Connolly, Garth Fowden, Denise Harvey, Gaïl Holst-Warhaft, Elizabeth Key Fowden, Peter Mackridge, John Raffan, Philip Ramp, Pavlos Sfyroeras, Avi Sharon, Liadain Sherrard & Andrew Watson, Limni, Evia: Denise Harvey, 2007.

Papadiamandis, Alexandros, *The Shores of Twilight*, trans. Belica-Antonia Koubareli, Athens: Kostas and Eleni Ouranis Foundation, 2000.

Papadiamantis, Alexandros, *Love in the Snow*, trans. J. Coggin & Z. Lorenzatos, Athens: Domos, 1993.

Papadiamantis, Alexandros, *Tales from a Greek island*, trans. Elizabeth Constantinides, Baltimore: John Hopkins University Press, 1987.

Papadiamantis, Alexandros, *The Murderess*, trans. Peter Levi, London: Writers and Readers, 1983. Also London: Loizou Publications, 1995 and New York: New York Review of Books, 2010.

Papadiamantis, Alexandros, *The Murderess*, trans. George X. Xanthopoulides, ed. Kyriakos Ntelopoulos, London: Doric Publications, 1977.

MODERN
GREEK
CLASSICS

C.P. CAVAFY
Selected Poems
BILINGUAL EDITION
Translated by David Connolly

Cavafy is by far the most translated and well-known Greek poet internationally. Whether his subject matter is historical, philosophical or sensual, Cavafy's unique poetic voice is always recognizable by its ironical, suave, witty and world-weary tones.

STRATIS DOUKAS
A Prisoner of War's Story
Translated by Petro Alexiou
With an afterword by Dimitris Tziovas

Smyrna, 1922: A young Anatolian Greek is taken prisoner at the end of the Greek–Turkish War. A classic tale of survival in a time of nationalist conflict, *A Prisoner of War's Story* is a beautifully crafted and pithy narrative. Affirming the common humanity of peoples, it earns its place among Europe's finest anti-war literature of the post-WWI period.

ODYSSEUS ELYTIS
1979 NOBEL PRIZE FOR LITERATURE
In the Name of Luminosity and Transparency
With an Introduction by Dimitris Daskalopoulos

The poetry of Odysseus Elytis owes as much to the ancients and Byzantium as to the surrealists of the 1930s and the architecture of the Cyclades, bringing romantic modernism and structural experimentation to Greece. Collected here are the two speeches Elytis gave on his acceptance of the 1979 Nobel Prize for Literature.

NIKOS ENGONOPOULOS

Cafés and Comets After Midnight and Other Poems
BILINGUAL EDITION

Translated by David Connolly

Derided for his innovative and, at the time, often incomprehensible modernist experiments, Engonopoulos is today regarded as one of the most original artists of his generation. In both his painting and poetry, he created a peculiarly Greek surrealism, a blending of the Dionysian and Apollonian.

M. KARAGATSIS

The Great Chimera
Translated by Patricia Barbeito

A psychological portrait of a young French woman, Marina, who marries a sailor and moves to the island of Syros, where she lives with her mother-in-law and becomes acquainted with the Greek way of life. Her fate grows entwined with that of the boats and when economic downturn arrives, it brings passion, life and death in its wake.

ANDREAS LASKARATOS

Reflections
BILINGUAL EDITION

Translated by Simon Darragh
With an Introduction by Yorgos Y. Alisandratos

Andreas Laskaratos was a writer and poet, a social thinker and, in many ways, a controversialist. His *Reflections* sets out, in a series of calm, clear and pithy aphorisms, his uncompromising and finely reasoned beliefs on morality, justice, personal conduct, power, tradition, religion and government.

MARGARITA LIBERAKI
The Other Alexander
Translated by Willis Barnstone and Elli Tzalopoulou Barnstone

A tyrannical father leads a double life; he has two families and gives the same first names to both sets of children. The half-siblings meet, love, hate, and betray one another. Hailed by Albert Camus as "true poetry," Liberaki's sharp, riveting prose consolidates her place in European literature.

ALEXANDROS RANGAVIS
The Notary
Translated by Simon Darragh

A mystery set on the island of Cephalonia on the eve of the Greek Revolution of 1821, this classic work of Rangavis is an iconic tale of suspense and intrigue, love and murder. *The Notary* is Modern Greek literature's contribution to the tradition of early crime fiction, alongside E.T.A. Hoffman, Edgar Allan Poe and Wilkie Collins.

EMMANUEL ROÏDES
Pope Joan
Translated by David Connolly

This satirical novel and masterpiece of modern Greek literature retells the legend of a female pope as a disguised criticism of the Orthodox Church of the nineteenth century. It was a bestseller across Europe at its time and the controversy it provoked led to the swift excommunication of its author.

ANTONIS SAMARAKIS
The Flaw
Translated by Simon Darragh

A man is seized from his afternoon drink at the Cafe Sport by two agents of the Regime by car toward Special Branch Headquarters, and the interrogation that undoubtedly awaits him there. Part thriller and part political satire, *The Flaw* has been translated into more than thirty languages.

GEORGE SEFERIS
1963 NOBEL PRIZE FOR LITERATURE
Novel and Other Poems
BILINGUAL EDITION

Translated by Roderick Beaton

Often compared during his lifetime to T.S. Eliot, George Seferis is noted for his spare, laconic, dense and allusive verse in the Modernist idiom of the first half of the twentieth century. Seferis better than any other writer expresses the dilemma experienced by his countrymen then and now: how to be at once Greek and modern.

ILIAS VENEZIS
Serenity
Translated by Joshua Barley

Inspired by the author's own experience of migration, the novel follows the journey of a group of Greek refugees from Asia Minor who settle in a village near Athens. It details the hatred of war, the love of nature that surrounds them, the hostility of their new neighbours and eventually their adaptation to a new life.

GEORGIOS VIZYENOS
Thracian Tales
Translated by Peter Mackridge

These short stories bring to life Vizyenos' native Thrace, a corner of Europe where Greece, Turkey and Bulgaria meet. Through masterful psychological portayals, each story keeps the reader in suspense to the very end: Where did Yorgis' grandfather travel on his only journey? What was Yorgis' mother's sin? Who was responsible for his brother's murder?

GEORGIOS VIZYENOS
Moskov Selim
Translated by Peter Mackridge

A novella by Georgios Vizyenos, one of Greece's best-loved writers, set in Thrace during the time of the Russo-Turkish War, whose outcome would decide the future of southeastern Europe. *Moskov Selim* is a moving tale of kinship, despite the gulf of nationality and religion.

NIKIFOROS VRETTAKOS
Selected Poems   BILINGUAL EDITION
Translated by David Connolly

The poems of Vrettakos are firmly rooted in the Greek landscape and coloured by the Greek light, yet their themes and sentiment are ecumenical. His poetry offers a vision of the paradise that the world could be, but it is also imbued with a deep and painful awareness of the dark abyss that the world threatens to become.

AN ANTHOLOGY
Greek Folk Songs
BILINGUAL EDITION

Translated by Joshua Barley

The Greek folk songs were passed down from generation to generation in a centuries-long oral tradition, lasting until the present. Written down at the start of the nineteenth century, they became the first works of modern Greek poetry, playing an important role in forming the country's modern language and literature.

AN ANTHOLOGY
Rebetika: Songs from the Old Greek Underworld
BILINGUAL EDITION

Edited and translated by Katharine Butterworth & Sara Schneider

The songs in this book are a sampling of the urban folk songs of Greece during the first half of the twentieth century. Often compared to American blues, rebetika songs are the creative expression of the *rebetes*, people living a marginal and often underworld existence on the fringes of established society.